YOU AGAIN

You Again
(*or* You, Again)

A BOOK OF LOVE-HATE STORIES

collated and edited
by Kirsten Irving and Jon Stone

sidekickBOOKS

First published in 2022 by
SIDEKICK BOOKS
www.sidekickbooks.com

Printed by
ImprintDigital

Typeset in Libre Baskerville and Raleway

Copyright of text and images remains with the authors.

Kirsten Irving and Jon Stone have asserted their right to be identified as the editors of this work under Section 77 of the Copyright, Designs and Patents Act 1988.

Sidekick Books asserts that under Section 30A of the Copyright, Designs and Patents Act 1988 this work should be treated as pastiche, and that reasonable use of excerpts from copyrighted works therefore does not infringe copyright.

All rights reserved.

No part of this book may be reproduced, stored in a retrieval system or transmitted in any form without the written permission of Sidekick Books.

Cover design / typesetting by Jon Stone
ISBN: 978-1-909560-30-7

Overleaf: *Murder of Agamemnon* by Pierre-Narcisse Guérin

> As the best wine makes the sharpest vinegar, truest love can turn into truest nemesis.

— Nikhil Kushwaha, *Heart of Bullets*

> This universe, no matter how vast, will never be big enough for you and I to coexist.

— Optimus Prime, *Transformers: Fall of Cybertron*

CONTENTS

"The idea of the love-hate relationship ..."   *13*

SAPPHO
I loved you, Atthis ...   *17*
A. A. MILNE
from Winnie-the-Pooh   *18*
RAMONA HERDMAN
Ever After House   *21*
CAMILLE RALPHS
She Learns to Count   *22*
CAROLINE GILFILLAN
Sheila   *23*
DANTE GABRIEL ROSSETTI
Sister Helen   *24*
SOMERSET MAUGHAM
from Of Human Bondage   *36*
KATHERINE PETERS-COOK
The words 'I love you'   *37*

"Suppose, though, that rather ..."   *38*

CLAIRE ORCHARD
Hedging   *41*

PAUL STEPHENSON
The Misoscopist   *43*
MARY SHELLEY
from Frankenstein   *44*
WALT WHITMAN / ÉMILE VERHAEREN
Infinity Songs   *46*
ALICE CARPENTER
The Big Bad   *48*
G. K. CHESTERTON
from The Flying Stars   *51*
ANONYMOUS
Concerning the Arts   *54*
CHRISTINA ROSSETTI / VITA SACKVILLE-WEST
Bittergarden   *57*

"Then, of course, there is ..."   *58*

ROBERT LOUIS STEPHENSON
from Kidnapped   *62*
LARA FRANKENA
Borneo   *63*
JULIA ROSE LEWIS
Suburbiton   *64*
RAMONA HERDMAN
Bacon   *67*
OVID (tr. HENRY T. RILEY)
Midas   *68*

LARA FRANKENA
Her Psychic Arm — 69

CLAIRE CROWTHER
A Sweet Accord — 70

WES LEE
Thinking about my corpse — 73

NATHANIEL HAWTHORNE
from The Birth-Mark — 74

LOTTE MITCHELL REFORD
The Lincoln Memorial — 76

CARL NICHOLLS
RMS Olympic, to her sister — 78

EMILY BRONTË
Wuthering Heights — 80

"Is it defeatist ...?" — 81

Notes and Acknowledgments — 82
Biographies — 83

This book contains a threaded introduction. It begins here and resumes at points throughout.

THE idea of the love-hate relationship is at least as old as Catullus[1], who declared "*Odi et amo* (I hate and I love)" and wrote of his friends and lovers with equal parts spite and devotion, often in the space of the same brief poem. Love-hate relationships are a staple of modern dramatic fiction, whether they occur between romantic partners, family members, colleagues or rivals. In Japanese popular culture, the word *tsundere* (ツンデレ) – a portmanteau of *tsuntsun*/ツンツン (disgusted or grumpy) and *deredere*/デレデレ (lovey-dovey or affectionate) – is used for a stock character type. This alternately hyper-critical and doting figure is as central to *shōjo* manga (comics aimed at girls and young women) as Columbina is to Italian *commedia dell'arte*, or the Police Constable to Punch and Judy. Westerners may be more familiar with the use of the word 'frenemy' to describe such real-life dynamics, as well as in fan discourse.

---

[1] See Stone, J. and Irving, K (2017) *Bad Kid Catullus*, London: Sidekick Books.

Why then, if these relationships are so common, is the 'love-hate story' not more widely embraced? Why are love-hate plots and subplots so often resolved into love stories, or stories of differences being set aside? Perhaps because without some form of positive resolution, they cannot be said to be stories at all – or rather, they're stories which have become stuck at a crossroads. And if that's the case, perhaps it also reveals what is most limiting and artificial about traditional stories: that they insist on moving us on, discarding the paradoxes and contradictions that dominate large portions of our lives in favour of closure. In doing so, they repeatedly set us up for disappointment by having us believe that conflicted feelings are always a prelude to the revelatory moment, rather than a mortal condition.

Accordingly, when we suspend stories by stopping them at their mid-point, or extract from them a sequence of events which lack either set-up or payofff, we can imbue the result with the character of poetry, since poetry finds purchase in the midst of conflict, tension and ambiguity. Unsurprising, then, that many of the 'stories' that follow are actually poems, or linger in the hinterland between poem and story.

That there is such a proliferation of emotional conflict in our everyday lives, while explicable in other ways, suggests something rather discomforting: that love only exists as a counterbalancing force. That what we call 'love' might be a potion we concoct to pour into the well of fear and frustration within each of us, to keep it from boiling over. Love's intensity – its concentration – is, therefore, a direct reflection of how firmly our propensity to hate presses us, how sharply it digs into us, how steadily it ballasts us. We love, in that case, so that we are not animated solely by anticipation of danger or loss.

If this is so, it's little wonder that when our capacity to love is strained or exhausted a tremendous imbalance threatens to reveal itself. In such circumstances, the object of our love may not always become the object of our wrath, but the sensations we associate with love are very easily reconfigured into ones of suffering, shame and despair. This turmoil we then record, as best we're able, in art, song and literature.

SAPPHO

Ἄτθι, σοὶ δ' ἔμεθεν μὲν ἀπήχθετο
φροντίσδην, ἐπὶ δ' Ἀνδρομέδαν πότᾳ

Ἔρος δηὖτέ μ' ὁ λυσιμέλης δόνει,
γλυκύπικρον ἀμάχανον ὄρπετον

I loved you, Atthis, once, long years ago! The thought of me is hateful now, I know;	*trans:* (JMO)
Hateful my face is to thee, Hateful to thee beyond speaking, Atthis, who fliest from me.	(HDS)
Again, Love, slackener of limbs, inflames me: sweetbitter, irresistible creepling. Crawling thing.	(ASK/JP/BC)

"In this two-part fragment, Sappho gives us an image of overwhelming power in Eros, which she experiences (it would seem) with the departure of a young favourite for a rival ... I propose that the creature Sappho had in mind in this poem was the bee, that creature which carried both honey and a sting, pleasure and pain."
—Bonnie McLachlan, 'What's Crawling in Sappho Fr. 130'

A. A. MILNE
from Winnie-the-Pooh

First of all he said to himself: "That buzzing-noise means something. You don't get a buzzing-noise like that, just buzzing and buzzing, without its meaning something. If there's a buzzing-noise, somebody's making a buzzing-noise, and the only reason for making a buzzing-noise that I know of is because you're a bee."

Then he thought another long time, and said: "And the only reason for being a bee that I know of is making honey."

And then he got up, and said: "And the only reason for making honey is so as I can eat it." So he began to climb the tree.

He climbed and he climbed and he climbed, and as he climbed he sang a little song to himself. It went like this:

> *Isn't it funny*
> *How a bear likes honey?*
> *Buzz! Buzz! Buzz!*
> *I wonder why he does?*

Then he climbed a little further ... and a little further ... and then just a little further. By that time he had thought of another song.

It's a very funny thought that, if Bears were Bees,
They'd build their nests at the bottom of trees.
And that being so (if the Bees were Bears),
We shouldn't have to climb up all these stairs.

He was getting rather tired by this time, so that is why he sang a Complaining Song. He was nearly there now, and if he just stood on that branch ...

Crack!

"Oh, help!" said Pooh, as he dropped ten feet on the branch below him.

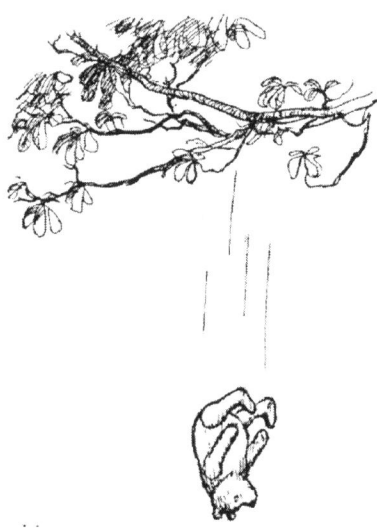

"If only I hadn't –" he said, as he bounced twenty feet on to the next branch.

"You see, what I meant to do," he explained, as he turned head-over-heels, and crashed on to another branch thirty feet below, "what I meant to do –"

"Of course, it was rather –" he admitted, as he slithered very quickly through the next six branches.

"It all comes, I suppose," he decided, as he said good-bye to the last branch, spun round three times, and flew gracefully into a gorse-bush, "it all comes of liking honey so much. Oh, help!"

He crawled out of the gorse-bush, brushed the prickles from his nose, and began to think again.

RAMONA HERDMAN
Ever After House

I went riding all night on Tear Me Apart Road.
—Mark Doty

I stay in and ache for Tear Me Apart Road.
I'm half out the window, sucking at stars,
humming sirens. I have myself well in hand,
pink and clean as the last little pig. But O

my soul is a witch still, lean crone,
shallow-rooted, half out of her head
always after being a red-eyed hare running
down the gutter to Drown Me Fen.

I have this palace for my good behaviour.
I brush my hair a hundred times. Bird-women
sing on Tear Me Apart Road: it winds up
Fling Me Mountain. It starts just outside.

CAMILLE RALPHS
She Learns to Count

She saw your kindness poke fun at her crying eye just once.

Not more than twice, she watched your honesty swear blind it did not know her.

Three times – three at most – she saw your cleverness look doe-eyed at a huckster of the first degree.

It might have been four times she witnessed your good humour screaming like a kettle in her favourite restaurant.

Was it five times she recognised your decency amid the crowd howling for tabloid blood?

There was a sixth occasion, she supposes, when she spotted your ambition on the sofa with a spliff and gaping case of wine.

No way could it be seven times she, shopping with your generosity, paid up with everything she had.

Nor eight times, surely, that she watched your self-control professing palpitations of the heart to someone new!

Nine times ... Nine times she did not think she knew, or thought she could not know.

Ten times she heard someone in love with you deny the constitution of your soul.

CAROLINE GILFILLAN
Sheila

Buzzing through Islington, singing *Wherever I Lay My Hat* through bubbles of Special Brew, you were a charmer, a hustler who winked at girls at traffic lights. You told me your landlady was a tiger in the sack, that your flat would soon be worth a cool million. Those things were true but not everything was. I fell for your crooked grin, your freckles, your blag. You smelled of Persil and oranges. And fags, always fags – forty a day, puffing while you told me your affair with my Aussie ex 'just happened'. I wanted to skin you for your feeble shoulder shrug. I ended it, but more than once you turned up steaming, beating on my door at night, insisting I was your closest friend. *It was my Irish mother*, you wailed decades later, cuddling your plump King Charles spaniel, begging for vodka in that filthy mobile home. Your teeth had fallen out. I bundled you off to rehab in a taxi but you scarpered. Two years later you were dead. I'll remember you for your dusty Ford Capri, for the pink fluffy dice, for cursing in a Greek rainstorm, for your green eyes, round as gobstoppers, your soft mouth telling lies, spilling kisses.

DANTE GABRIEL ROSSETTI
Sister Helen

"Why did you melt your waxen man
Sister Helen?
To-day is the third since you began."
"The time was long, yet the time ran,
Little brother."
(O Mother, Mary Mother,
Three days to-day, between Hell and Heaven!)

"But if you have done your work aright,
Sister Helen,
You'll let me play, for you said I might."
"Be very still in your play to-night,
Little brother."
(O Mother, Mary Mother,
Third night, to-night, between Hell and Heaven!)

"You said it must melt ere vesper-bell,
Sister Helen;
If now it be molten, all is well."
"Even so,—nay, peace! you cannot tell,
Little brother."
(O Mother, Mary Mother,
O what is this, between Hell and Heaven?)

"Oh the waxen knave was plump to-day,
Sister Helen;
How like dead folk he has dropp'd away!"
"Nay now, of the dead what can you say,
Little brother?"
(O Mother, Mary Mother,
What of the dead, between Hell and Heaven?)

"See, see, the sunken pile of wood,
Sister Helen,
Shines through the thinn'd wax red as blood!"
"Nay now, when look'd you yet on blood,
Little brother?"
(O Mother, Mary Mother,
How pale she is, between Hell and Heaven!)

"Now close your eyes, for they're sick and sore,
Sister Helen,
And I'll play without the gallery door."
"Aye, let me rest,—I'll lie on the floor,
Little brother."
(O Mother, Mary Mother,
What rest to-night, between Hell and Heaven?)

"Here high up in the balcony,
Sister Helen,
The moon flies face to face with me."
"Aye, look and say whatever you see,
Little brother."

(O Mother, Mary Mother,
What sight to-night, between Hell and Heaven?)

"Outside it's merry in the wind's wake,
Sister Helen;
In the shaken trees the chill stars shake."
"Hush, heard you a horse-tread as you spake,
Little brother?"
(O Mother, Mary Mother,
What sound to-night, between Hell and Heaven?)

"I hear a horse-tread, and I see,
Sister Helen,
Three horsemen that ride terribly."
"Little brother, whence come the three,
Little brother?"
(O Mother, Mary Mother,
Whence should they come, between Hell and Heaven?)

"They come by the hill-verge from Boyne Bar,
Sister Helen,
And one draws nigh, but two are afar."
"Look, look, do you know them who they are,
Little brother?"
(O Mother, Mary Mother,
Who should they be, between Hell and Heaven?)

"Oh, it's Keith of Eastholm rides so fast,
Sister Helen,

For I know the white mane on the blast."
"The hour has come, has come at last,
Little brother!"
(O Mother, Mary Mother,
Her hour at last, between Hell and Heaven!)

"He has made a sign and called Halloo!
Sister Helen,
And he says that he would speak with you."
"Oh tell him I fear the frozen dew,
Little brother."
(O Mother, Mary Mother,
Why laughs she thus, between Hell and Heaven?)

"The wind is loud, but I hear him cry,
Sister Helen,
That Keith of Ewern's like to die."
"And he and thou, and thou and I,
Little brother."
(O Mother, Mary Mother,
And they and we, between Hell and Heaven!)

"Three days ago, on his marriage-morn,
Sister Helen,
He sicken'd, and lies since then forlorn."
"For bridegroom's side is the bride a thorn,
Little brother?"
(O Mother, Mary Mother,
Cold bridal cheer, between Hell and Heven!)

"Three days and nights he has lain abed,
Sister Helen,
And he prays in torment to be dead."
"The thing may chance, if he have pray'd,
Little brother!"
(O Mother, Mary Mother,
If he have pray'd, between Hell and Heaven!)

"But he has not ceas'd to cry to-day,
Sister Helen,
That you should take your curse away."
"My prayer was heard,—he need but pray,
Little brother!"
(O Mother, Mary Mother,
Shall God not hear, between Hell and Heaven?)

"But he says, till you take back your ban,
Sister Helen,
His soul would pass, yet never can."
"Nay then, shall I slay a living man,
Little brother?"
(O Mother, Mary Mother,
A living soul, between Hell and Heaven!)

"But he calls for ever on your name,
Sister Helen,
And says that he melts before a flame."
"My heart for his pleasure far'd the same,
Little brother."

(O Mother, Mary Mother,
Fire at the heart, between Hell and Heaven!)

"Here's Keith of Westholm riding fast,
Sister Helen,
For I know the white plume on the blast."
"The hour, the sweet hour I forecast,
Little brother!"
(O Mother, Mary Mother,
Is the hour sweet, between Hell and Heaven?)

"He stops to speak, and he stills his horse,
Sister Helen;
But his words are drown'd in the wind's course."
"Nay hear, nay hear, you must hear perforce,
Little brother!"
(O Mother, Mary Mother,
What word now heard, between Hell and Heaven?)

"Oh he says that Keith of Ewern's cry,
Sister Helen,
Is ever to see you ere he die."
"In all that his soul sees, there am I
Little brother!"
(O Mother, Mary Mother,
The soul's one sight, between Hell and Heaven!)

"He sends a ring and a broken coin,
Sister Helen,

And bids you mind the banks of Boyne."
"What else he broke will he ever join,
Little brother?"
(O Mother, Mary Mother,
No, never join'd, between Hell and Heaven!)

"He yields you these and craves full fain,
Sister Helen,
You pardon him in his mortal pain."
"What else he took will he give again,
Little brother?"
(O Mother, Mary Mother,
Not twice to give, between Hell and Heaven!)

"He calls your name in an agony,
Sister Helen,
That even dead Love must weep to see."
"Hate, born of Love, is blind as he,
Little brother!"
(O Mother, Mary Mother,
Love turn'd to hate, between Hell and Heaven!)

"Oh it's Keith of Keith now that rides fast,
Sister Helen,
For I know the white hair on the blast."
"The short short hour will soon be past,
Little brother!"
(O Mother, Mary Mother,
Will soon be past, between Hell and Heaven!)

"He looks at me and he tries to speak,
Sister Helen,
But oh! his voice is sad and weak!"
"What here should the mighty Baron seek,
Little brother?"
(O Mother, Mary Mother,
Is this the end, between Hell and Heaven?)

"Oh his son still cries, if you forgive,
Sister Helen,
The body dies but the soul shall live."
"Fire shall forgive me as I forgive,
Little brother!"
(O Mother, Mary Mother,
As she forgives, between Hell and Heaven!)

"Oh he prays you, as his heart would rive,
Sister Helen,
To save his dear son's soul alive."
"Fire cannot slay it, it shall thrive,
Little brother!"
(O Mother, Mary Mother,
Alas, alas, between Hell and Heaven!)

"He cries to you, kneeling in the road,
Sister Helen,
To go with him for the love of God!"
"The way is long to his son's abode,
Little brother."

(O Mother, Mary Mother,
The way is long, between Hell and Heaven!)

"A lady's here, by a dark steed brought,
Sister Helen,
So darkly clad, I saw her not."
"See her now or never see aught,
Little brother!"
(O Mother, Mary Mother,
What more to see, between Hell and Heaven?)

"Her hood falls back, and the moon shines fair,
Sister Helen,
On the Lady of Ewern's golden hair."
"Blest hour of my power and her despair,
Little brother!"
(O Mother, Mary Mother,
Hour blest and bann'd, between Hell and Heaven!)

"Pale, pale her cheeks, that in pride did glow,
Sister Helen,
'Neath the bridal-wreath three days ago."
"One morn for pride and three days for woe,
Little brother!"
(O Mother, Mary Mother,
Three days, three nights, between Hell and Heaven!)

"Her clasp'd hands stretch from her bending head,
Sister Helen;

With the loud wind's wail her sobs are wed."
"What wedding-strains hath her bridal-bed,
Little brother?"
(O Mother, Mary Mother,
What strain but death's, between Hell and Heaven?)

"She may not speak, she sinks in a swoon,
Sister Helen,—
She lifts her lips and gasps on the moon."
"Oh! might I but hear her soul's blithe tune,
Little brother!"
(O Mother, Mary Mother,
Her woe's dumb cry, between Hell and Heaven!)

"They've caught her to Westholm's saddle-bow,
Sister Helen,
And her moonlit hair gleams white in its flow."
"Let it turn whiter than winter snow,
Little brother!"
(O Mother, Mary Mother,
Woe-wither'd gold, between Hell and Heaven!)

"O Sister Helen, you heard the bell,
Sister Helen!
More loud than the vesper-chime it fell."
"No vesper-chime, but a dying knell,
Little brother!"
(O Mother, Mary Mother,
His dying knell, between Hell and Heaven!)

"Alas! but I fear the heavy sound,
Sister Helen;
Is it in the sky or in the ground?"
"Say, have they turn'd their horses round,
Little brother?"
(O Mother, Mary Mother,
What would she more, between Hell and Heaven?)

"They have rais'd the old man from his knee,
Sister Helen,
And they ride in silence hastily."
"More fast the naked soul doth flee,
Little brother!"
(O Mother, Mary Mother,
The naked soul, between Hell and Heaven!)

"Flank to flank are the three steeds gone,
Sister Helen,
But the lady's dark steed goes alone."
"And lonely her bridegroom's soul hath flown,
Little brother."
(O Mother, Mary Mother,
The lonely ghost, between Hell and Heaven!)

"Oh the wind is sad in the iron chill,
Sister Helen,
And weary sad they look by the hill."
"But he and I are sadder still,
Little brother!"

(O Mother, Mary Mother,
Most sad of all, between Hell and Heaven!)

"See, see, the wax has dropp'd from its place,
Sister Helen,
And the flames are winning up apace!"
"Yet here they burn but for a space,
Little brother! "
(O Mother, Mary Mother,
Here for a space, between Hell and Heaven!)

"Ah! what white thing at the door has cross'd,
Sister Helen?
Ah! what is this that sighs in the frost?"
"A soul that's lost as mine is lost,
Little brother!"
(O Mother, Mary Mother,
Lost, lost, all lost, between Hell and Heaven!)

SOMERSET MAUGHAM
from Of Human Bondage

"I don't care a damn if you like me or not. I'm sick of being made a blasted fool of. You're jolly well coming to Paris with me on Saturday or you can take the consequences."

Her cheeks were red with anger, and when she answered her voice had the hard commonness which she concealed generally by a genteel enunciation.

"I never liked you, not from the beginning, but you forced yourself on me, I always hated it when you kissed me. I wouldn't let you touch me now, not if I was starving."

Philip tried to swallow the food on his plate, but the muscles of his throat refused to act. He gulped down something to drink and lit a cigarette. He was trembling in every part. He did not speak. He waited for her to move, but she sat in silence, staring at the white tablecloth. If they had been alone he would have flung his arms round her and kissed her passionately; he fancied the throwing back of her long white throat as he pressed upon her mouth with his lips. They passed an hour without speaking, and at last Philip thought the waiter began to stare at them curiously. He called for the bill.

KATHERINE PETERS-COOK
The words 'I love you'

are a tool, of course, and a weapon (a weapon of self-defence?) as well as a key being turned, as well as an exposed wound (neat or jagged?), as well as a proffered pearl (freshly harvested?), as well as a judgement, as well as a gasp for air, as well as an incantation. You may, upon hearing them, feel as if you are being led into or out of a cage. You may feel as if you are being interrogated, or called up as an expert witness, or sat down in front of a puzzle box. You may feel as if a metal probe has been inserted into you, or a private item taken from your drawer and put on display. Once said, the words 'I love you' might linger briefly, or they might buzz about your head till you swat them away. They might vanish immediately, so that you doubt their being said, or they might leave a painful splinter in your ear. You may choose to seal them in a jar and keep that jar about you at all times, or else take it to your lab and study the words 'I love you' under a microscope, never learning if they're living or dead. You might ride out to meet them with your own words in retinue, as welcome party or counterattack. You might even respond with the very same words, so that the two sets of triplets meet in the air and face each other down. You may feel you hear these words too often. On the other hand, you may feel sure you'll never know their like again.

"The Ministry of Peace concerns itself with war, the Ministry of Truth with lies, the Ministry of Love with torture and the Ministry of Plenty with starvation. These contradictions are not accidental, nor do they result from ordinary hypocrisy: they are deliberate exercises in doublethink."

— George Orwell, *1984*

Suppose, though, that rather than love being the opposite of hate, *both* have something to do with control, that they are a knife and fork worked in unison, or two fists with 'love' and 'hate' tattooed on the knuckles. This might explain why they've been found to light up the same parts of the brain (namely the putamen and the insula).

Except that as much as these emotions are forces we are able to bring to bear, our propensity to feel and act upon them impulsively means that we often find ourselves manipulated through them. At any one time, therefore, we may not be sure whether we're summoning forth love in order to take command of ourselves and others, or having love drawn from us (like a scarf from a magician's sleeve) by some greater power. We may not be sure whether we are wielding hate as a whip, or having it fastened around us (like a spiked collar) by some handler. And though we insist on our autonomy and independence in most situations, often it is more convenient to believe the opposite – that we are ensnared – rather than recognise our own attempts to exert control (one might even say: to cast a spell) by channeling these emotions.

We can only really understand the forces in play by turning them over in our hands and examining them, which we do in part by writing about them. Consider actor Christopher Lee's account of the shifting power dynamic between himself and the role he is most famous for, from his 1977 autobiography:

"It brought me a name, a fan club and a second-hand car, for all of which I was grateful. It also, if I may be forgiven for saying so, brought me the blessing of

Lucifer. Count Dracula may escape, but not the actors who play him. Eventually I made too many. I am not ashamed of him. My feelings about Stoker's character never radically altered throughout seven films. Simply, it was aesthetically depressing to see the films step by step deteriorate. Scars Of Dracula *was truly feeble. With* The Satanic Rites Of Dracula *I reached my irrevocable full stop. At the age of 50 I took the firm decision to Draculate no more."*

There is much in this that reminds us of the contradictions that characterise the kind of romantic relationship which typically lasts a few years: the honeymoon period, the painful stagnation, the assurance that there is something at the core of it all which has never faltered. Lee does us the service of demonstrating that issues of control and autonomy arise wherever we develop attachments – or perhaps that attachments are, at their root, ways in which we both cede and seize command of our own lives.

CLAIRE ORCHARD
Hedging

I will not sentimentalise hedgerows, any more than I would rhapsodise about motorway earthworks, or glamorise skyscrapers, although I'll admit to watching films with titles like *Heart of the Hedgerow* and envying those who, in the winter months, when all is dormant and quiet, go out with axe and billhook and methodically slash a row of sleeping saplings, slicing their narrow stems almost in bleeding two before bending them over, cracking them against their nature, strapping them down.

I am attracted, and at the same time repelled, by the clusterings of tender shoots that appear at these sites of deliberate mutilation. And, I remind myself, every hedgerow is a border line, designed to keep some creatures in and others out. Almost thirty thousand linear miles thread the landscape, forming fences, marking ancient parish boundaries.

I will not idealise that first smallholder who, centuries ago, while clearing the wilderness for grazing animals, saw in that final teetering row of spindly hazel an opportunity to dominate and domesticate. I will not romanticise stakes severed from living trees and driven into hard ground, sinewy binders sliced to length and woven through, repurposed to confine, their strength used against them.

Even knowing this early farmer's prediction came to pass, that this first injured row did heal itself, as would those that followed. Even knowing the tightest of fetters will eventually rot, falling to earth in damp fragments; that new growth will spurt from the wounds, a thickening that in turn will become a teeming, familial network of roots eager to bind soil and capture rainwater, a weathered refuge for wild creatures, sturdy sequester of carbon, superhighway for bees. Constant collector of fallen sunlight and snow.

PAUL STEPHENSON
The Misoscopist

I prefer to stay home and avoid beauty. I like to order in. Japanese food most nights. Boy or girl, I never look the delivery person in the eye in case their eyes are amazing. I eat miso soup. Or should I say drink? Miso soup most days. Mondays miso, Tuesdays miso … and that's my week. When I stir it the tiny particles of soya look like the universe. A hot, cloudy, white-speckled universe. I drink down the stars. But it's the little cubes of tofu that really do it for me, the way they bobble and swirl like planets moving fast around a sun. And I don't need a telescope, only my tongue.

I never go out between meals in case it's Spring and the trees are in bud. The cherry blossom in Kyoto would kill me. I'm always on the lookout for new places to order from, but when I'm not sat waiting for home delivery, I try to read, tell myself to spend more time reading. I read about the history of miso, gender theories on miso, the rituals of miso-making, rainy-day things to do with miso. I don't agree with the latest thinking, the way miso has been re-imagined. Ask me what I think and I'm unlikely to tell you. Unless, like me, you've a taste for distaste and a penchant for being reclusive. No, I'm not fussed about all the salt and … sorry, I'd better get that, it's the door.

MARY SHELLEY
from Frankenstein

It was on a dreary night of November that I beheld the accomplishment of my toils. With an anxiety that almost amounted to agony, I collected the instruments of life around me, that I might infuse a spark of being into the lifeless thing that lay at my feet. It was already one in the morning; the rain pattered dismally against the panes, and my candle was nearly burnt out, when, by the glimmer of the half-extinguished light, I saw the dull yellow eye of the creature open; it breathed hard, and a convulsive motion agitated its limbs.

How can I describe my emotions at this catastrophe, or how delineate the wretch whom with such infinite pains and care I had endeavoured to form? His limbs were in proportion, and I had selected his features as beautiful. Beautiful! Great God! His yellow skin scarcely covered the work of muscles and arteries beneath; his hair was of a lustrous black, and flowing; his teeth of a pearly whiteness; but these luxuriances only formed a more horrid contrast with his watery eyes, that seemed almost of the same colour as the dun-white sockets in which they were set, his shrivelled complexion and straight black lips.

The different accidents of life are not so changeable as the feelings of human nature. I had worked hard for nearly two years, for the sole purpose of infusing life into an inanimate body. For this I had deprived myself of rest and health. I had desired it with an ardour that far exceeded moderation; but now that I had finished, the beauty of the dream vanished, and breathless horror and disgust filled my heart. Unable to endure the aspect of the being I had created, I rushed out of the room and continued a long time traversing my bedchamber, unable to compose my mind to sleep. At length lassitude succeeded to the tumult I had before endured, and I threw myself on the bed in my clothes, endeavouring to seek a few moments of forgetfulness. But it was in vain; I slept, indeed, but I was disturbed by the wildest dreams.

WALT WHITMAN / ÉMILE VERHAEREN
Infinity Songs

Far removed, stretched out beneath the stars
I celebrate myself
and dreadful voices fill the sky,
fanning out as they pass one another.

I loafe and invite my Soul
to the endless dewy woods.

Here and there, lights crouched in groups of four
grizzle and nip at the darker shadows
and become undisguised and naked.

They rage and snatch
for every atom belonging to me.

I lean and loafe at my ease, observing:
houses and rooms are full of perfumes
from the infinite swamps and flatlands.

The dogs of autumn, of the wind.
The black evening echoes.
A spear of summer grass.

The moon sits twinned in the mirror.
It has no taste of the distillation
—it is odorless. I am in love with it.

The atmosphere is not a perfume.
It is for my mouth forever.
I am mad for it to be in contact with me.

I will go to the bank by the wood,
and what I assume you shall assume;
roadways that stretch out like sails
through the shadows and horrors of the night,
as good belong to you.

ALICE CARPENTER
The Big Bad

Yōdō was dead, and not before time. It took six seasons of *Bullet Melody* to bury him. Over one hundred episodes of surrogate swordfights, infiltrations, random cruelties, kidnappings, doomsday devices and calmly cruel speeches. Yōdō had betrayed his former comrades without a thought. He had even sacrificed his sister Shin, selling her to the tyrant Faceturner in exchange for a blade that could cut between worlds.

Our little group had watched dully as hot-headed hero Tama banished her schoolgirl self and trained to meet her destiny. Under her mentor's gaze and her friends' support, she took on the mind games and mazes the demon king set for her, finally reaching Yōdō's dark keep. At the cursed gates, she 'died' for three episodes after angel-knives monsooned down on her gang. Luckily, an old prophecy saw her resurrected with ten times the power, a lightning staff, huge blue hair and a much shorter skirt.

Some people love a Messiah figure, but none of us really rooted for Tama, nor her tiresome sidekick, the water sprite Himatsu (Droplet). We knew that neither one could die. We scrambled instead to cosplay Kashira, the scruffy ninja exiled from her clan, who fell in with Tama after saving her life. Kashira was an *idiot savant*, easily distracted by food and cats. She would pause mid-parry to "nyaan" at a tabby, absently blocking the enemy's blade as she fussed her furry friend.

Yōdō's death scene took up half a season. To clear the way for Tama's glory, Kashira was cheated, knocked out for five episodes following a soul blast from a cackling lieutenant. Each episode of the final fight seemed to open and close with Tama panting on the ground, while the demon king mused, "How pitiful." But in the end, as the public demands, the Ordinary Schoolgirl came back from the brink to turn him unequivocally to ash.

Up until this point, I had found *Bullet Melody*'s main antagonist smug, untested and overpowered. I bristled at Yōdō's unexplained knowledge and despaired of countless plotholes (one cannot tailor a nuclear attack to avoid certain buildings). I even felt for Tama as Yōdō loomed and she staggered beneath the weight of her new power, afraid of disappearing or disappointing her father, right up until the end. I was relieved when Yōdō fell and stayed down.

But when Season 7 began, the peace was exhausting. The elastic had snapped. I missed the threat, the unspecified danger, the slick double-crossings, the lust for power that smoked from Yōdō's fingers, the cutaways to his acolytes, the pullback out of his spy-pool and the pan across to his smiling grey lips. I missed his cold orders, his serene executions, his casual obsession with destroying a schoolgirl.

Other villains tried their hands, but each one was either a dilute Yōdō or a useless amalgam that rose and fell before the leaves turned. His death changed everything. After Yōdō, Tama was too strong, too confident. She was a battle veteran, outskilling her mentor, and her rivals were now her friends. She could never return to school or her mall job. Nobody would make her eyes go wide again.

G. K. CHESTERTON
from The Flying Stars
(A detective addresses a thief)

He sparkles from head to heel, as if clad in ten million moons; the real moon catches him at every movement and sets a new inch of him on fire. But he swings, flashing and successful, from the short tree in this garden to the tall, rambling tree in the other, and only stops there because a shade has slid under the smaller tree and has unmistakably called up to him.

"Well, Flambeau," says the voice, "you really look like a Flying Star; but that always means a Falling Star at last."

The silver, sparkling figure above seems to lean forward in the laurels and, confident of escape, listens to the little figure below.

"It was clever to come from Canada just a week after Mrs. Adams died, when no one was in a mood to ask questions. It was cleverer to have marked down the Flying Stars and the very day of Fischer's coming. But there's no cleverness, but mere genius, in what followed. Stealing the stones, I suppose, was nothing to you. You could have done it by sleight of hand in a hundred other ways besides that pretence of putting a paper donkey's tail to Fischer's coat. But in the rest you eclipsed yourself."

The silvery figure among the green leaves seems to linger as if hypnotised, though his escape is easy behind him; he is staring at the man below.

"I want you to give them back, Flambeau, and I want you to give up this life. There is still youth and honour and humour in you; don't fancy they will last in that trade. Men may keep a sort of level of good, but no man has ever been able to keep on one level of evil. That road goes down and down. The kind man drinks and turns cruel; the frank man kills and lies about it. Many a man I've known started like you to be an honest outlaw, a merry robber of the rich, and ended stamped into slime. Maurice Blum started out as an anarchist of principle, a father of the poor; he ended a greasy spy and tale-bearer that both sides used and despised. Harry Burke started his free money movement sincerely enough; now he's sponging on a half-starved sister for endless brandies and sodas. Lord Amber went into wild society in a sort of chivalry; now he's paying blackmail to the lowest vultures in London. Captain Barillon was the great gentleman-apache before your time; he died in a madhouse, screaming with fear of the 'narks' and receivers that had betrayed him and hunted him down. I know the woods look very free behind you, Flambeau; I know that in a flash you could melt into them like a monkey. But some day you will be an old grey monkey, Flambeau. You will sit up in your free forest cold at heart and close to death, and the tree-tops will be very bare."

Everything continued still, as if the small man below held the other in the tree in some long invisible leash; and he went on:

"Your downward steps have begun. You used to boast of doing nothing mean, but you are doing something mean tonight. You are leaving suspicion on an honest boy with a good deal against him already; you are separating him from the woman he loves and who loves him. But you will do meaner things than that before you die."

Three flashing diamonds fell from the tree to the turf. The small man stooped to pick them up, and when he looked up again the green cage of the tree was emptied of its silver bird.

ANONYMOUS
Concerning the Arts

In terms of advancing human self-knowledge and dignity, the greatest impediment to the success of the arts industries is without doubt the high status accorded to the artist. You already know this. The successful writer or artist becomes a symbol solely of success, of the cultural metanarrative that divides people into strivers and spongers, wealth creators and idle beneficiaries. Their work is gradually absorbed into a conglomerate sense of what all art is and does – a permissible range of messages which we have already heard, about how life is brief and strange and wondrous, misery miserable, greed evil, love all-conquering, and so on and so forth.

Some resist this fate but few escape it completely. Whatever incendiary intentions the artist may have started out with, success and status act as a crack bomb-disposal squad. The very concept of being countercultural, anarchic or disruptive has now been safely integrated into mainstream culture, and the freedom to paradoxically enjoy institutional recognition while flying the flag of revolution is just one more privilege that the successful are allowed to flaunt before the rest.

The unsuccessful artist does not escape unscathed either. I should know, being one. For one thing, all unsuccessful artists are lumped with the job of becoming successful, of becoming a symbol of what most of them have set out to oppose or improve upon. Those that try to evade this obligation are reminded of it every time their practice as an artist is brought up in casual conversation, since they are asked, of course, not about what they are in the midst of investigating but to what degree their work has been institutionally beatified. Who has spent money on it? How many lowly publicists, designers, distributors and administrators have been tasked with delivering it to the masses? A true artist, after all, is someone of status; they must have people working for them. If you don't (so the logic goes) you can only say you aspire to be an artist.

Worse still, the unsuccessful artist is lumped with the job of loving themselves. Their attention is constantly redirected towards their own being, and only by genuflecting before that *being* are they allowed to thrive in their work. They would do better, in fact, to attend to that being as scrupulously as possible than to expend the bulk of their time and effort on outwardly-directed thought, experimentation and enquiry. They must secure for that being alliances, favour, admiration, sympathy, visibility, and other vectors of influence – to the point where many, for the sake of efficiency, make these duties a central component of the art itself.

From this there emerges a circuit – a self-enclosed network of subcultures which affect to be primarily concerned with transgression, agitation and plurality, but which are, in fact, utterly preoccupied with stature, continuity and consensus. The individual ambition to wander off into the mists is blunted – best to stay within the safety of the encampment. This because the artist, as a figure, is afforded too much respect, is regarded as someone whose purpose is not to do, but to be. It is a mean trick played upon those who are among the least inclined to love themselves, to put them at odds with their own nature, to make the game they play unwinnable.

English writer Malcolm Lowry (1909-1957) speaks of the outcome in his short poem 'Success is like some horrible disaster':

Fame like a drunkard consumes the house of the soul
Exposing that you have worked for only this –
Ah, that I had never known such a treacherous kiss
And had been left in darkness forever to work and fail.

CHRISTINA ROSSETTI / VITA SACKVILLE-WEST
Bittergarden

Love is gone with all its roses,
    Its sun and perfumes and warm flowers,
    Flowers that English poets sing,
    Humble sweetly-smelling stocks,
    Daffodils and hollyhocks.

Yea, love's chilly self is going,
    And love comes which is yet colder:
    Hoar-frost, wallflowers, creepers red,
    Lavender and borage blue;
    Love was all that ever grew.

Then, of course, there is the tremendous energy that tends to be bound up in conflicted emotions, and in relationships which are soaked in conflict. That energy is frequently destructive – tragically so – but can also be directed to more productive ends, to the point where we sometimes consider the potential for destruction to be an acceptable price.

Take the case of film director Werner Herzog and actor Klaus Kinski – the latter an individual who became notorious for the damage and abuse he wreaked on those around him, as well as his frequent delusions of godliness. Of the making of 1972's *Aguirre, Wrath of God*, Herzog recalls:

"As usual, [Kinski] didn't know his lines properly and was looking for a victim. He started shouting 'You swine!' at the camera assistant for grinning at him, demanding I fire him on the spot. I said, 'No. I'm not going to fire him — we're 17,000 feet up in the Andes, and the whole crew would quit out of solidarity.'

Kinski walked off, packed all his things and was absolutely serious about quitting and leaving at once — he'd already broken his contract 40 or 50 times … I told him I had a rifle and that he'd only make it as far as the first bend before he had eight bullets in his head — the ninth one would be for me."

Herzog further reports that on the set of 1982's *Fitzcarraldo,* the indigenous people working as extras came to him and offered to kill Kinski:

"I needed Kinski for a few more shots, so I turned them down. I have always regretted that I lost that opportunity."

He would go on to say, in the 1999 documentary *Klaus Kinski – Mein Liebster Feind* (*My Best Enemy*), that all of this "was worthwhile for what you see on the screen. Who cares if every grey hair on my head I call 'Kinski'? … and you know, he was one of the few people I ever learned anything from."

Herzog himself is famously cavalier, prone to existential reverie, and known for making extreme demands of his crew in the name of art (the production of *Fitzcarraldo* involved dragging an entire paddle steamer over a mountain). What if he had all but required the explosive tensions inherent in his relationship with Kinski in order to make the impossible possible?

There is at least some indication that Kinski (who died in 1991) might have thought so. His opinions of Herzog – those on record – are full of bitterness and loathing:

"Herzog is a miserable, hateful, malevolent, avaricious, money-hungry, nasty, sadistic, treacherous, cowardly creep [...] he should be thrown alive to the crocodiles! An anaconda should strangle him slowly! A poisonous spider should sting him and paralyse his lungs! The most venomous serpent should bite him and make his brain explode! No — panther claws should rip open his throat — that would be much too good for him!"

And yet he was also reported to have said the following:

"Nobody is going to buy the book if I say nice things about you, Werner."

The world of art and literature is littered with similar examples of memorable works emerging from the heat of broken or torturous marriages and affairs. Even as liberal society is rightly committed to a program of detoxification – emphasising our capacity to defuse volatile situations, mitigate the effects of trauma and escape damaging relationships – there is an accompanying sense that we risk losing out on valuable insights into our natures if we can no longer bear the pain of battling our tormentors.

ROBERT LOUIS STEPHENSON
from Kidnapped

"David!" he cried. "Are ye daft? I cannae draw upon ye, David. It's fair murder."

"That was your look-out when you insulted me," said I.

"It's the truth!" cried Alan, and he stood for a moment, wringing his mouth in his hand like a man in sore perplexity. "It's the bare truth," he said, and drew his sword. But before I could touch his blade with mine, he had thrown it from him and fallen to the ground. "Na, na," he kept saying, "na, na — I cannae, I cannae."

At this the last of my anger oozed all out of me; and I found myself only sick, and sorry, and blank, and wondering at myself. I would have given the world to take back what I had said; but a word once spoken, who can recapture it? I minded me of all Alan's kindness and courage in the past, how he had helped and cheered and borne with me in our evil days; and then recalled my own insults, and saw that I had lost for ever that doughty friend. At the same time, the sickness that hung upon me seemed to redouble, and the pang in my side was like a sword for sharpness. I thought I must have swooned where I stood."

LARA FRANKENA
Borneo

We are lucky: a female orangutan is sat on the kerb in the car park while her baby gambols nearby. We are warned not to get too close.

Farther up the dirt trail other orangutans are gathered at a feeding centre, including an adult male. Adult males, we are told, are extremely intolerant of crying babies, and will approach. *If your baby starts to cry,* the guide says, *back up, quickly, and go back down the trail.*

There I am, pregnant again, holding my three-year-old's hand, my one-year-old in a sling on my back. *You see,* my husband hisses, *it's not just me.*

JULIA ROSE LEWIS
Suburbiton

Is she my chrysanthemum? Mums come in the colours bronze, cabernet, garnet, tinkerbell and more. Single and semidouble blooms. Among the four mares there are mums, plum blossoms, bamboo and orchids. Mums are susceptible to mites. She is changing her head, from globular form to reflex form to pompom form to the anemone form to the spoon form to the spider form. The spider form folds and unwinds itself the spider wife as one ant does another. Of the daisy family indeed. Her life perennial if withstanding the wind and winging spring. Not an airplane. Please she says not an airplane not an airplane not yet. The Farmers' Almanac tells me that mums like loamy soils and more if following the hum of summer and fall. She is dear as the wind, daughter of the wind, windflower to an enemy if enemies are literally flowing to following it is only denoting a bunch of ribbons, bands, and ants intimidating as they are plural. I can not remember if the pragmatist said a blooming buzzing confusion if marigolds and cosmos are related. Mums are susceptible to mildew. As a lion is turning old and mild in the rainwater, morifolium is susceptible to mingling together with other flowers.

I am mean. I mean the email did relate to marigolds and cosmos. Spam is might not may be a symptom about to be blossoming against the email. I want to say against nausea. Spam means motion sickness in the same way scopolamine means against motion sickness. It is not blossoming in the stomach. I dream about scopolamine and the next morning she sends me an email about spam. Spam is not only manners. It is blooming and summoning more blooms to come to from ammonia. The dream is related to marigolds and cosmos. Scopolamine also known as high yellow scene will mean I am a mean employee. It is demanding mind to mind. I know in the dream there are two off-label uses for scopolamine: one is reducing saliva in terminally sedated patients and the other is not given to discussion. It used to be used for anaesthesia. It is also known as hyoscine, not as high yellow scenes of blossoms. I mean spam. I mean scopolamine if it is signifying the common mean small confusion. It is a nonselective antagonist if given. As long as the email means no one thing, no one thinking thing created this monsoon.

The house as a green house so new is continuous with twin. A landrace breed, a sister to other lanthanides, domestic, she is dedicated to the sand, water, land, and pepper-related diseases. As the pungency increases, so the history of this plant was stressed by increased water salinity, nutrition, insects, erratic watering, light or illness. Open pollinated might lead to phenomenology of the feral pepper. The third is not given. She clings to the fish the next square over from here. Discontinuous us. Didymium as praseodymium as yellow and green and neodymium forms a residue. Her lips are ringed in dark grey. So now the green fish and the twin fish indistinguishable as sisters go fish! She is ductile. She is dedicated to the aquifer, rare earth metals and sand. Scars relate to heat as small brown lines. Capsaicin can be found in the vesicles surrounding the seeds, concentrate to white or yellow or fluorescing in violet light. Her eyes are outlined in a light light jalapeño green. As jalapeños are susceptible to tobacco mosaic virus, tomato spotted wilt virus, pepper mottle virus and root-knot nematodes to name. Continuous us know that capsicum annum is numbing the distance. The fifth is given.

RAMONA HERDMAN
Bacon

These travelling days, it's everywhere –
limp in baps in the train's buffet bar,
frazzled stars over every deli salad,
spreadeagled under the breakfast heatlamps.

I spend a lot of time alone
and one thing I keep to myself is that,
after a decade of abstinence,
the smell of butchers' shops has changed

from the gag of bloodsnot down the back of my throat
to the best roast ever welcoming me home,
a made feast, to signal the satisfying tug
of meat in teeth. Smells now like a soulmate.

I could do it without anyone knowing.
I could do anything.

OVID (tr. HENRY T. RILEY)
Midas

Bacchus, having punished the Thracian women for the murder of Orpheus, leaves Thrace. His tutor, Silenus, having become intoxicated, loses his companions, and is brought by some Phrygian peasants to King Midas. Midas sends him to Bacchus, on which the God, in acknowledgment of his kindness, promises him whatever favour he may desire. Midas asks to be able to turn everything that he touches into gold.

Silenus again becomes intoxicated and loses his companions, and again is brought by some Phrygian peasants to Midas. Again, Midas sends him to Bacchus, on which the God, in acknowledgment of his kindness, promises him whatever favour he may desire. Midas asks to be able to turn all of his gold into women.

For a third time, Silenus loses his companions, and is brought by the same group of Phrygian peasants to Midas. Once more, Midas sends him to Bacchus, on which the God, in acknowledgment of his kindness, promises him whatever favour he may desire. Midas asks to be able to turn all of his women into flasks of wine.

LARA FRANKENA
Her Psychic Arm

Tapping two fingers against her left forearm, my friend uses muscle testing to uncover past-life traumas that trouble me presently. One revelation after another sees us from Lisbon to Porto in her rental car – a manual, no less.

The locus appears to be a difficult ex, with whom I've been entangled several times, primarily in France and Asia. Usually, I kill myself, apart from an incident in the 900s when he killed me.

Once, we had four children. *What happened?* my friend asks herself. *Did they die? Which one? The first ... second ... third ... fourth ... Oh! They all died!*

CLAIRE CROWTHER
A Sweet Accord

Hewidow he is. / Herhusband I call him.
— 'A Pair of Three'

i. Noticing odd things while sleepy . . .

Notably: only life or death matters keep us awake
        and here he is sitting up in a gyre of panic.

Notably: he's fingering the pink embroidery on the bedspread.
        He thinks his first wife bought this warm cover.

Notably: the alternative to panic is proposal.
        Does he propose to examine those old diaries?

Notably: what he wrote long ago is treasure:
        tiny books
        dated spines

ii. What his diary might say if I were to write it . . .

2 Sunday: Varying views on life & death keeping me awake:
        who widowed . . . who widow-wed . . .

who widowered . . .

15 Saturday: Ju? Remember this bedspread? Chosen for its
        pink embroidered water avens?
        & there's something else . . .

19 Wednesday: we were never obnoxious with each other! as
        I might be now if I insist on
        thinking of you.

27 Thursday: Thinking of you.

27 Thursday: Must go now.

31 Sunday: Oncewife?

31 Sunday: Listen! Dark is different! Dark matter has
        no sound.
        You said there was nothing.

31 Sunday: There's only light.
        I was sunwed I won't unwed.
        You're something!

31 Sunday: Are you even here?
        Can't you watch with me a while?

iii. For what it's worth . . .

Fortuitously
>some matters are curiously clear in the small hours.

For example
>that I remember while you

Forget
>that this bedspread with its distinctive drooping heads of water avens
>was chosen by me *Livewife* to celebrate
>your proposal – though that was a while back.

Forgotten!
>Proposals are life-changing!
>But beloved you felt yours might be life
>-threatening
>and so when you think of it don't panic

For
>while I'm here and she's there you need never

Forego
>our

Forbearance
>while, life and death apart, we're awake again . . .

WES LEE
Thinking about my corpse

Thinking about *she* there. Still dressing her in women's clothes. Still dressing her as a girl. Even before the furnace we are squeezed into shape.

I brought plain white knickers to the undertaker with my mother's clothes. And now I wonder if he struggled her into them or tossed them knowing we would not rifle through?

Thinking about the sweet smell of lilies, and flies and Walter Mosley's Pet Fly how he used it as a metaphor for his internalised self hatred.

How Samuel Pepys clutched the corpse of Queen Catherine of Valois, pulled her dry sticks toward him and kissed her lips.

Thinking about the generous wet sack. Moisture. Bag of dissolving hope.

Thinking about Marlon Brando in *The Missouri Breaks* dragging the corpse from the coffin by the lapels. Ice scattering. The terror of the bystanders.

NATHANIEL HAWTHORNE
from The Birth-Mark

"One day, very soon after their marriage, Aylmer sat gazing at his wife with a trouble in his countenance that grew stronger until he spoke.

"Georgiana," said he, "has it never occurred to you that the mark upon your cheek might be removed?"

"No, indeed," said she, smiling; but perceiving the seriousness of his manner, she blushed deeply. "To tell you the truth it has been so often called a charm that I was simple enough to imagine it might be so."

"Ah, upon another face perhaps it might," replied her husband; "but never on yours. No, dearest Georgiana, you came so nearly perfect from the hand of Nature that this slightest possible defect, which we hesitate whether to term a defect or a beauty, shocks me, as being the visible mark of earthly imperfection."

"Shocks you, my husband!" cried Georgiana, deeply hurt; at first reddening with momentary anger, but then bursting into tears. "Then why did you take me from my mother's side? You cannot love what shocks you!"

To explain this conversation it must be mentioned that in the centre of Georgiana's left cheek there was a singular mark, deeply interwoven, as it were, with the texture and substance of her face. Its shape bore not a little similarity to the human hand, and Georgiana's lovers were wont to say that some fairy at her birth hour had laid her tiny hand upon the infant's cheek, and left this impress there in token of the magic endowments that were to give her such sway over all hearts. Had she been less beautiful – if Envy's self could have found aught else to sneer at – Aylmer might have felt his affection heightened by the prettiness of this mimic hand, now vaguely portrayed, now lost, now stealing forth again and glimmering to and fro with every pulse of emotion that throbbed within her heart. But seeing her otherwise so perfect, he found this one defect grow more and more intolerable with every moment of their united lives.

At all the seasons which should have been their happiest, he invariably and without intending it, nay, in spite of a purpose to the contrary, reverted to this one disastrous topic. Trifling as it at first appeared, it so connected itself with innumerable trains of thought and modes of feeling that it became the central point of all. Georgiana soon learned to shudder at his gaze. It needed but a glance with the peculiar expression that his face often wore to change the roses of her cheek into a deathlike paleness, amid which the crimson hand was brought strongly out, like a bass-relief of ruby on the whitest marble.

LOTTE MITCHELL REFORD
The Lincoln Memorial

When I first see the Lincoln Memorial I am impressed. The plinth he sits on is huge. He is perched atop it like a toddler in a high chair. I text to tell you your fingers remind me of Lincoln's, or rather the Lincoln Memorial's fingers remind me of yours. My hands are a mess. All chewed up.

I am ~~trapped~~ in the USA 2.5 years before I see the Lincoln Memorial, and the big plinth doesn't fix anything. You show me art hoes on your phone, because that is what we are now, art hoes. They all have pastel hair. Before I ~~run away to~~ catch my flight for Mexico the second time, Tali tells me she thinks some people are just depressive by nature, as well as depressed.

She tells me this in a dark apartment ~~she hates~~ in a college town ~~we both hate~~. She tells me as she colours my hair. My hands on your phone, I say yes, yes, no, no, no, no, she looks boring. The bleach burns my scalp where Tali has rubbed too hard. In Mexico, Christmas means endless unsmashed piñatas and sunshine parades through snow made of dish soap.

I wonder if all the piñatas are empty. Does being depressive by nature mean we depress ourselves, or that nothing is good enough, or is it pure biology? In Mexico there is a waterfall stood perfectly still. From its lip I can see fields of agave – neat lines of green spikes. A tequila farm.

A farm to supply Pier 1 with succulents. In Mexico, I text to tell you I hope your fish are all dead. On a long car ride, the sky and desert are the biggest things I have ever seen. I know this can't be true, because I have seen the curve of a horizon and been in other, flatter deserts.

I conclude that I am pretending to impress myself. I conclude that I only grew a personality to make someone ~~like you~~ love me. I conclude I am nothing but careful curation with a girl hiding underneath.

I conclude that it is ~~being walled in by~~ the wide ring of mountains that makes everything look so large. I buy a bottle of mezcal from a roadside stall. I wonder who the girl is and what she likes to drink. I conclude that it was just the shape of Lincoln's fingernails that reminded me of you. I just wish, for a moment, I could stand completely still.

CARL NICHOLLS
RMS Olympic, *to her sister*

Of nights like yours are coral made.
Abandoned? You truly have no idea.
When the call came I came to you. I tried.
A hundred knots out, they turned me back.
Those in peril, they believed,
would sooner glimpse God's foot in the deep,
than climb aboard their death-ship's twin.

After the war, like a good girl does,
I went back into commerce.
But business foundered and fuel was precious.
Bleeding money,
Old Reliable got her cards.
It took two years to break and scatter me:
fittings restrung for a hotel staircase,
windows brightening a factory
panels arrayed in a country church.

You were never so collected.
After the loss of your surface beauty,
you settled into your brine suite, your lore,
your blue-green shrine.
The century turned. I gained graffiti.
You: another film, a documentary.
Told and retold, you will yet outlive me,
the dullest of your long-doused lamps
retrieved and prized as pearls.

EMILY BRONTË
Wuthering Heights

This is certainly a beautiful country! In all England, I do not believe that I could have fixed on a situation so completely removed from the stir of society. A perfect misanthropist's Heaven – and Mr. Heathcliff and I are such a suitable pair to divide the desolation between us.

Will you say so, Mr. Heathcliff?

Mr. Heathcliff, this is the talk of a madman.

I sha'n't speak to you, Mr. Heathcliff.

Mr. Heathcliff, *let* me go home!

Mr. Heathcliff, you *are* miserable. Lonely, like the devil, and envious like him. *Nobody* loves you – *nobody* will cry for you when you die! I wouldn't be you!

(It was too late: Heathcliff had caught hold of her.)

"She had some horses.

She had some horses she loved.
She had some horses she hated.

These were the same horses."
—Joy Harjo

Is it defeatist to think that the two cannot be separated? After all, we strive to eradicate hate from our lives and to see love triumph in as many ways as we're able to imagine. Perhaps it's better, though, to think in terms of an internal balance – a sort of poise that is made possible only by permitted ourselves both passions. By doing so, we may find we are better able to account for the role conflict plays in our lives, and to use that conflict as the basis for the ongoing exercise of self-discovery.

NOTES AND ACKNOWLEDGMENTS

The translators of the individual lines of Sappho are John Myers O'Hara, Henry De Vere Stacpoole, A. S. Kline, Jim Powell and Bliss Carmen.

'Infinity Songs' is a collage of 'Song of Myself' by Walt Whitman and 'Oneindig' ('Infinitely') by Émile Verhaeren.

'Bittergarden' is a collage of 'Bitter for Sweet' by Christina Rossetti and 'The Garden' by Vita Sackville-West.

An earlier version of Wes Lee's 'Thinking about my corpse' appeared in *The Poetry New Zealand Yearbook 2019* (Massey University Press).

Works by A. A. Milne, G. K. Chesterton, Somerset Maugham, Mary Shelley, Nathaniel Hawthorne and Emily Brontë have been heavily abridged for this volume.

All unattributed pieces either come from anonymous sources or are the work of the editors.

BIOGRAPHIES

EMILY BRONTË (1818-1848) was a Yorkshire-born poet and novelist, and the sister of fellow writers Charlotte and Anne Brontë. Brontë's most famous novel is *Wuthering Heights*, which was only considered a masterpiece after her death.

ALICE CARPENTER is a collaborative mixed-media artist interested in travel and folklore. She was born near Bradford and works as an illustrator and photographer's assistant.

G. K. CHESTERTON (1874-1936) was a writer, critic and philosopher, known as the prince of paradox. He was hugely prolific, completing novels, poems, short stories, essays and plays, including the Father Brown mysteries and the metaphysical spy thriller *The Man Who Was Thursday*.

CLAIRE CROWTHER has published four poetry collections and five pamphlets. She was awarded a Poetry Book Society Recommendation for Spring 2020 for her current collection *Solar Cruise*. She is Deputy/Reviews Editor of *Long Poem Magazine* and teaches poetry for the Oxford University Creative Writing Diploma.
⊕ clairecrowther.co.uk

LARA FRANKENA lives in London. Her poems have appeared in publications such as *Poetry News*, *Ink Sweat & Tears* and *Shot Glass Journal* and were longlisted for the 2021 and 2022 Erbacce Prizes.

CAROLINE GILFILLAN has published five collections of poetry. She won the Yeovil Poetry Prize in 2019, and her collection *Yes*, was judged best poetry book in the East Anglian Awards. Her work has recently been published in *Prole* and *Bloody Amazing*.
🌐 carolinegilfillan.co.uk   🐦 poetcaroline

NATHANIEL HAWTHORNE (1804-1864) was an American gothic and dark romantic writer, best known for his anti-Puritan novel *The Scarlet Letter*. Herman Melville, a close friend, dedicated his novel *Moby-Dick* to Hawthorne, "In token of my admiration for his genius".

RAMONA HERDMAN's recent publications are *Glut* (Nine Arches Press), *A warm and snouting thing* (The Emma Press) and *Bottle* (HappenStance Press). Ramona lives in Norwich and is a committee member for Café Writers.
🐦 ramonaherdman

Originally from the UK, WES LEE lives in New Zealand. Her work has appeared in *The Stinging Fly*, *The London Magazine*, *Poetry London*, *New Writing Scotland*, *Australian Poetry Journal* and *Best New Zealand Poems*. She has won a number of awards for her writing, including the Poetry New Zealand Prize 2019, awarded by Massey University Press.

JULIA ROSE LEWIS is the author of *Phenomenology of the Feral* (KFS, 2017), *High Erratic Ecology* (KFS, 2020), and *The Hen Wife* (Contraband, 2020). She and Nathan Hyland

Walker co-authored *The Velvet Protocol* (KFS, 2022). James Miller and she co-authored *Strays* (HVTN, 2017).

📷 lilysbarnmate   🐦 lilysbarnmate

W. SOMERSET MAUGHAM (1874-1965) was an English writer who worked for the British Secret Service during the Second World War. *Of Human Bondage*, a semi-autobiographical novel, is considered his finest work.

A. A. MILNE (1882-1956) was a novelist, playwright, *Punch* contributor and the author of the *Winnie The Pooh* series of children's books. The books were based on his son's soft toys and Pooh's name came from Winnipeg, a female bear at London Zoo.

LOTTE MITCHELL REFORD is usually a poet, currently working on a memoir about sickness and starving medieval saints. They hold an MFA from Virginia Tech, and are about to embark on a PhD at GSU. Their work has been published in, among other places, *Copper Nickel*, *Spam*, and H*obart Pulp*. They have a dog called Robin. He is an angry rescue chihuahua. Their first pamphlet, *and we were so far from the sea of course the hermit crabs were dead*, was published in 2021 by Broken Sleep Books.

CARL NICHOLLS is a writer and essayist based in Glasgow. He is a former cemetery tour guide and his first poetry collection, *Sneeze*, explored the wit of gravestones.

CLAIRE ORCHARD is from Aotearoa New Zealand and is the author of poetry collection *Cold Water Cure*. Her work has featured in *Ōrongohau / Best New Zealand Poems*, *Landfall*, *Turbine / Kapohau*, *The Interpreter's House*, *Overground Underground* and *The Rialto*. 🌐 claireorchardpoet.com

OVID (43BC-17-18AD) was a Roman poet and a contemporary of Virgil and Horace. He was known as a great elegiac love poet, though his most famous work is *The Metamorphoses*, an epic poem across fifteen books. Ovid was banished by Augustus to Tomis (Constanța in present-day Romania) and described his treatment as *"carmen et error"* ("a poem and a mistake").

KATHERINE PETERS-COOK (1887-1922) was a poet and former cabaret dancer from Boston, Massachusetts. She published several volumes of work, including *The Reader Writes The Reader* and *See The Bells Fall*. Her final collection, *Here Lies The American*, was assembled from drafts found in her apartment.

CAMILLE RALPHS has two published pamphlets, *Malkin: An ellegy in 14 spels* (The Emma Press, 2015) and *uplifts & chains* (If A Leaf Falls Press, 2020), with another forthcoming in 2023. She writes the 'Averse Miscellany' column for *Poetry London*, conducts the 'Poem's Apprentice' interview series for *Poetry Birmingham Literary Journal* and is Poetry Editor at the *TLS*. 🐦 camilleralphs_

HENRY T. RILEY (1816-1878) was the son of an ironmonger in Southwark. He was educated at Cambridge and called to the bar, but moved into publishing, translating the works of Ovid, Plautus and Pliny the Elder, among other classical authors.

CHRISTINA ROSSETTI (1830-1894) was an English romantic poet. Born in London to an Italian family, she began writing as a young teenager, and published her most famous work, *Goblin Market & Other Poems*, aged 31. Its themes of sexual curiosity, anxiety and repression may have been influenced by her volunteer work at a refuge for former sex workers.

DANTE GABRIEL ROSSETTI (1828-1882) was a poet and painter, and a founding member of the Pre-Raphaelite Brotherhood of artists. He also illustrated books, providing the artwork for his sister Christina's famous poem 'The Goblin Market'.

VITA SACKVILLE-WEST (1892-1962) was an English novelist, columnist, garden designer, poet and diarist. She was the inspiration for the eponymous gender-fluid hero in *Orlando: A Biography*, written by her lover Virginia Woolf. In *Portrait of a Marriage*, her sexual memoir, she wrote, "It will be recognized that many more people of my type do exist than under the present-day system of hypocrisy is commonly admitted."

SAPPHO (c. 630-570 BC) was a lyric poet born on the Greek island of Lesbos. Her passionate homoerotic work, which survives today only in fragments, was cited by Plato, alluded to by Socrates and admired and emulated by the Roman poet Catullus.

MARY SHELLEY (1797-1851) was an English gothic novelist and liberal feminist reformist, whose most famous novel, *Frankenstein; or, The Modern Prometheus*, was completed when she was just twenty years old. She was one of the earliest science fiction writers, articulating her own trials in life through her characters.

PAUL STEPHENSON has published three pamphlets: *Those People* (Smith/Doorstop, 2015), *The Days that Followed Paris* (HappenStance, 2016) and *Selfie with Waterlilies* (Paper Swans Press, 2017). He co-edited *Magma* #70 on the theme of 'Europe'. Paul co-curates Poetry in Aldeburgh and lives between Cambridge and Brussels. He interviews poets at ⊕ paulstep.com.   paulstep456   stephenson_pj

ÉMILE VERHAEREN (1855-1916) was a prolific Belgian poet, art critic and multiple-times nominee for the Nobel Prize in Literature.

WALT WHITMAN (1819-1892) was an influential American writer known for popularising free verse, and who was subject to censure for poems deemed obscenely sensual.

THANK YOU FOR YOUR ATTENTION

THE HIPFLASK SERIES

is an improvised dance of unusual forms and genres, played out across four collaborative, pocket-sized collections. Each book comprises a selection of works that skirt close to (or cross the border into) poetic composition, revealing the dynamic relationship between poetry and other kinds of writing. The major theme of each is extrapolated from one or other of these key aspects of modern poetry – play, appropriation, subtext *and* conflict *– but the result is a series that occupies its own strange niche: mutant miscellanies, oddball assortments. Good for a nip or a slug or a long, deep swig.*

SIDEKICK BOOKS

is a London-based small press specialising in collaborative works and experiments in genre.